VOLUME #1

Second paperback edition November 2022

Book design by Andrew Rogers

ISBN 979-8-9872-5606-0 (paperback)
ISBN 979-8-9872-5605-3 (ebook)

www.sanchicatalina.com

Sanchi Catalina Volume 1 / Andrew Rogers --2nd ed.

Chapters

VIAN ST

Chapter 1

Viviana's Diary

Page 1 - First Day of my long Adventure

I find it ridiculous how a simple dare with my best friend has gotten me a job in another galaxy. I never would have thought I would leave my galaxy. My biggest dream of traveling was just to La. This will be a tremendous challenge, but I feel I'm up to it. I don't want to let my friends and family down after getting this crazy opportunity. The scariest factor is going completely by myself to another galaxy I've only come to find out recently.

I will be the first of my family to leave the planet and also the galaxy. I feel the training and classes the government put me through have prepared me well for travel. Some things they talked about in the classes felt more like horror stories. It seemed they were only trying to discourage me from going. I'm determined to see unknown places and worlds, even though I found about these other galaxies recently. This is going to be an exciting adventure where I will have a lot of things to talk about when I get back.

With the medicine and classes, I'm all set and know I can handle dealing with them. My first sight of them I stopped in shock but had my guide with me which calmed me down. She told me once again if I wanted to turn back. She reassured me that if I went, the ones I will be around were not from our galaxy which made things better. They live in harmony amongst everyone; she told me. I wish I could take pictures, but the classes told me not to. I would attract unwanted attention, even though I'm still attracting attention without trying.

I'm acting like I have traveled past Vatresia's Void when I've only gone through the universal space station. Just going through the station opened my eyes to a lot of things. Every person I looked at seemed to come from a place with different clothing. Some had odd color hair which I had never seen before. It was a very interesting sight to see many strange people. My

Ca'Vais Galaxy ID PHOTO
Viviana (Planet: Ca)
ID#152

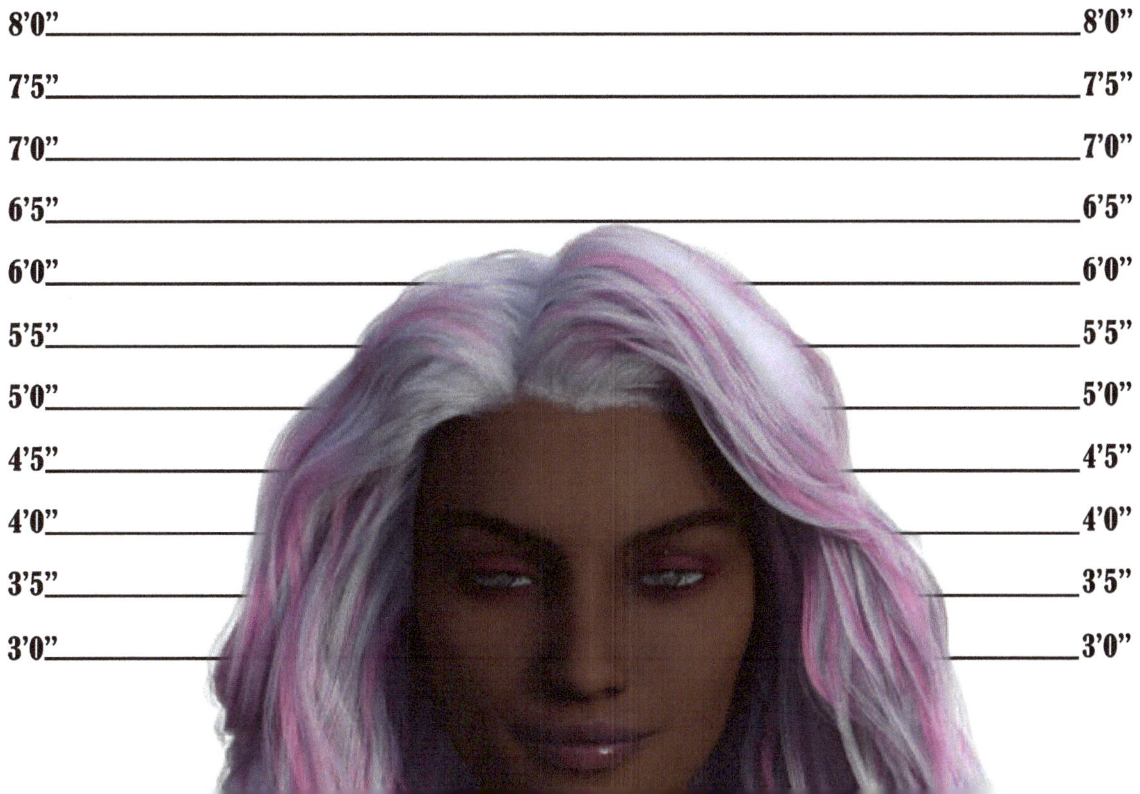
8'0" 8'0"
7'5" 7'5"
7'0" 7'0"
6'5" 6'5"
6'0" 6'0"
5'5" 5'5"
5'0" 5'0"
4'5" 4'5"
4'0" 4'0"
3'5" 3'5"
3'0" 3'0"

guide had left me by now so I'm walking around by myself. The very odd thing is that I'm the only of my kind I have seen sense my guide. I thought I would see at least one of my kind traveling.

Everyone looks different and wears different clothing from me, which now makes me feel that I'm the odd person. When I was boarding the ship, the lady kept looking at my ticket and saying if I was sure. There was no turning around now since I had made it this far.

This was my first-time walking into a ship of this size. I know it can definitely fit my entire city and the one next to it. There were nice seats and rooms that I'm guessing had beds in them for people to sleep. My seat number was very high. I knew I would not get a bed and room. By the time I found my area and seat, the ship had already taken off for space. Luckily, my seat wasn't around them, so I didn't have to worry about maybe one touching me. That would be a horrible nightmare. I had a window so I could see out into space, and traveling through the portal was the most beautiful thing I had ever seen. The government paid for my ticket, so I am very grateful. I know it was very expensive. I didn't have any money for food but was told that my contact would meet me once I got to the planet.

Even though people were communicating with each other, they mainly kept to themselves. No one has spoken to me yet, like there is some sort of secret rule. I know nothing about this galaxy besides the name Neetoi. I'm staying positive on the decision I have made, even if I had little choice. Doing that stupid dare and my parents eventually finding out was the only reason the government found out. Either travel to the galaxy or go to prison for violating the law and shaming my family were my only options. I don't have any regrets, and I know something good is going to come out of this.

I couldn't tell how long time had passed. I was starving and just stared out at what I assumed was the end of the portal we were going to travel through. The weird part was it never seemed to get bigger or smaller. I never felt we would ever get close to the end, and eventually the portal disappeared completely. Intercoms went off around the ship stating that we have entered the Neetoi galaxy and will soon approach the planet, Gavian. Once I get off the ship, I was told someone by the name of Tatiana will take me the rest of the way.

Getting off the ship and onto the planet wasn't a problem at all. The only thing that felt uncomfortable was the fact that there were more of them everywhere, and they seemed to have more control over the planet. Ignoring it and trying my best to avoid eye contact, but I know that I'm going to have to do it, eventually. I feel the medicine is wearing off but was told that it would last for my entire stay, so guessing it's just in my head. I walked up to the information booth to ask the person if she knew a person named Tatiana. She seemed to get very irritated with me and shooed me away, not helping

me at all. Those people seemed to want to help me, but I hurried away, looking down at the ground, not trying to catch eye contact. This was going to be a lot harder than I thought. Some of them now started pointing at me and talking amongst themselves.

This Tatiana person needs to hurry. I'm not feeling that comfortable around this area. I also need to find a rest and bath facility, which oddly is nowhere in sight. How do these people wash or relieve themselves? I grabbed my bag and picked a random road to explore. This is going to be so exciting writing about this new galaxy. I hope this planet Gavian has nice places to eat.

Chapter 2

Picking up the new girl

I can't believe this fool is going to hire someone, and then tell me at the very last moment to go pick them up. We barely see him and now he comes along telling me, Tatiana, you need to go pick up this new employee. Why me? How come I'm hearing about this so late, making me rush to this planet? I'm running late, but glad I made it on the same day. She better be lucky that she didn't have to spend the night on this filthy planet. I thought I was going to be serving drinks and listening to stories today. He's going to pay me well for this.

Ever since I got to this galaxy, it has been one stupid thing after another. These crazy isolated planets and moons with no actual security make it a haven for many criminals. Everyone who comes here has some story or secret they are running from. Running from their government or some criminal enterprise. This is going to be the first for me. I have seen no one apply to work here in this galaxy. There are so many better places in the universe, but this person would choose Neetoi. I hope this new girl is ready for the two-day trip

back to the Catalina. It will definitely be a culture shock for her.

Since I was told last minute, I made it to the station about a couple of hours late. No one looked lost in the area. Not knowing what she looked like, I looked for the lost and confused female that would wander around. It wasn't working, walking around looking at people. I walked over to one of the information booths to ask some questions.

 "Excuse me, have you seen a female walking around maybe lost or something?" I said to the man at the booth. He smiled, giving me the signal that he knew what I was talking about. He would not tell me because these Neetoi sleaze bags are always looking for a way to get money out of anyone. Everyone here is dirt poor and trying to find a way off this planet by any means. You also have these big violent gangsters trying to play ruler. For how long I've been living in this galaxy, I have heard no news or statements from the Neetoi government if it even still exists. It's probably some façade if exists and some big player runs it from the shadows, but what do I know I'm some bar girl at a crummy bar.

How much money I should try to start off with?

Knowing he's going to want more than the first offer, Neetois is nothing but pieces of crap. I pulled two notes out, making a third show a little for him to see. He took the two notes and pointed to the third in my pocket. I made a sad face like it was my last giving him the money. I hope this information is worth it.

"You're talking about that beautiful woman with the pink and grey hair. Everyone knew she was a lady Ca'Vais from that hair, and it looked like it was her first time here because she didn't cover it. It is mesmerizing to see that hair in the air. She avoided the men and walked down the street, but this was a while back. I don't know where she went. Bad thing is that this area isn't too safe for females of their kind. Since you gave me that extra note, I will tell you that the males and females of their kind do not get along so well." He looked around, making sure no one was listening, and continued, "Right here in this town there is an enormous refugee camp of males that settles here. I don't think they will be too nice to see a female walking around lost. What would make her come to a place with no one protecting her? Guess they are regular people where she's from. People would treat her like a queen here. Working here every day on this depressing planet that would be a dream come true to marry a Ca'Vais one day. You're cute, but you're not a lady Ca'Vais." I smiled. Idiot thought he was complimenting me. He gave me more information on her looks after telling more crap about his pathetic life, which I didn't want to hear. I looked in the direction that he said she walked and headed down the road. These men and their obsession with lady Ca'Vais. I guess Kadaway's manual was right. Knowing Pops, him and his love for Ca'Vais, I guess. I hope I will find her.

Chapter 3

First Impressions

Been walking around for a while now, still haven't found a rest area anywhere. I eventually found a tiny alley I could squeeze through and relieved myself I couldn't hold it anymore. Luckily, no one saw me. From everyone looking and pointing at me, I was glad no one saw me go down this alley. Now, I was thinking negative thoughts about everything. This was an ideal spot for a kidnapping. I should have been thinking about all these things before I boarded the ship. That lady was warning me because she knew of the dangers, and I was gullible. Leaving everything I know behind was a huge mistake. It was exciting at first, but the fear was now kicking in.

What subsided some of my fear was looking at all the unfamiliar faces and things I have never seen before. It wasn't beautiful here, compared to back home, but it was different and new to me. The stares and people pointing at me still made me feel uneasy, but I knew I was staring back at them. People have finally stopped trying to interact with me, realizing I would not speak to them. Some would still approach me, wanting to help, but wanted me to follow them. That was a big no go that I learned from my training. If that happens, I need to get away from them as fast as possible. What type of person is going to pick me up? I wish they would hurry and get here. Not having any money, I couldn't just turn around and go home. This is the only person I can depend on right now, and she isn't here.

"Hello, you seem to be lost. Can I help you?" A person stood behind me. I was shocked to hear the voice directly behind me. Turning to see that it was one of them now in front of me. I turned back around and started walking in the other direction.

"I wouldn't go down that way if I were you. It's dangerous, especially for people of your kind. You know your males are down there." As he said that, I froze in shock out of fear. I never even thought they

would live in this galaxy. Why didn't anyone say anything about this in training? I couldn't move from the fear overwhelming me, and not knowing if I should trust this person, seeing no proof.

"We get a few of your kind now and then and have heard the horror stories of your galaxy. I understand you might be afraid, but I'm not trying to harm you." He was now moving closer to me. I was now in total shock, not knowing if I should run. A male was right in front of me, but he wasn't my kind. Can I trust him or hope he is lying and continue down the path? Even if he is lying, what can be down that path that can help me? Too many thoughts raced through my head, making me give in and decide to trust this person.

"I'm from Ca'Vais and I'm trying to get to a place

called the Sanchi Catalina. Do you know where it is?" He was now in my face. I felt uneasy, but he kept smiling. I didn't want to be too defensive since he was helping me, so I gave a little smile back.

 "The Catalina, you say? You're very lucky! That's close to here. Come with me and I can give you a lift. Trust me, I have a couple of fellas that are going to the bar right now. You can be our bartender. I would love to get a drink from you." He laughed, but while he was talking, three other males appeared. Now there were four males around me. Having one of them around was bad enough, but now four. This was making me very uncomfortable, so I turned, heading back to the station, but one grabbed me. He wasn't nice, trying to pull me toward a door. I tried breaking free. While this was

going on, people around kept walking like nothing was happening. It shocked me that no one was helping. I was thinking about screaming. A person who seemed to be a security officer stood by, watching the event unfold.

 "Let go! I don't want to go with you!" I yelled at the one pulling my arm.

"Shut up! Stupid tool! You shouldn't have left your crappy planet! You know better! Now you will be of good use to your people!" He hit me in the head with his fist. It didn't knock me out, but it was my first time being hit, and it didn't feel good. Another male punched me two times in the stomach, causing me to drop all my things. Another grabbed my legs, and they carried me through the door, face up. I shouldn't have come to this place.

Chapter 4

The male Ca'Vais Camp

This place isn't that big, and I still can't find her anywhere. This shouldn't be that difficult looking for a female with pink and grey hair. You don't see that color around here with the local females. If we were in the Laop galaxy, that would be different. Here most of the hair colors are dark, and they don't wear clothes that a Ca'Vais would wear. Around here, with the male presence being this strong, it would be suicide. I wouldn't call this place a city, more like a huge enclave of refugee camps. It stinks here and there aren't any stores that don't look shady. Nothing but traffickers, criminals and poor residents live in this crap hole. I hope someone has not snatched her already. She would make them some good money.

Walking around was leading me nowhere. There was no decent person in this area to ask that wouldn't lie to me.

"Hello, are you lost or looking for someone?" A man said to me. Looking at him, I noticed a book in his hand that came from Ca'Vais, which was odd for him to have. Only females would have that type of book. It wasn't rare for males to have them, though.

"That's a pretty book you have there. Where did you get it?" Wanting to know how it got into his hands. He looked at me for a second, a little shocked I paid attention to it. Another guy walked up; I knew where this was heading, so the same ordeal probably happened to her, I'm guessing.

"There's a shop that sells this type of stuff down the street. I can take you there. Also, you'll see a lot of handsome Ca'Vais. Maybe you'll find your husband there." He smiled; I returned his smile, going along with his stupid plan. I could tell the other guy was a Ca'Vais, but the one holding the book wasn't. My weapon was cloaked, so I followed them, knowing if anything went bad, I had my weapon. Not wanting any trouble today was going to be out of the picture for me. Picking up a female in a dangerous area for females by a female, I don't think Pops thought this through.

They led me toward a door that looked nothing

like a store. The Ca'Vais seen my look and started getting more aggressive, shoving me as we got close to the door. He was getting on my nerves with all this touching. I let him push me, acting shocked that I was being mistreated. I could see that he was getting pleasure out of it. Once inside the room, I saw four females lying on the floor. Two had terrible bruises and the other two didn't look so bad. The one I was here to pick up wasn't that badly bruised. She looked up at me with a very pathetic look. Damn, I know she already regrets coming here.

He shoved me into the room for the last time.

I dropped and rolled forward, pulling out my gun, shooting him. The burst of shots went through his chest. Everyone watched in shock, seeing his lifeless body fall to the floor, blood splashing everywhere. That gave me enough time to shoot the two that were trying to escape. I killed one, but the other I could only shoot in the leg. He escaped, hopping out of the room. The one who brought me here was still in shock, with blood on his face. He finally was catching up to what had transpired. I pointed my gun in his face, speeding his thoughts up. "Look, I understand you are trying to make a quick

profit, but this one works with me. I will take the other ladies with me, but if you have a problem, we can talk it out." I was ready to fire if he wanted to waste my time any longer. He quickly agreed, knowing that it was his only option. I knew once he got out of my sight, he was going to go get his group and come looking for us. Also, the one that hopped out of the room would not let that slide. We had little time.

"Okay, listen up. We are not out of this mess yet. They are going to come looking for us. This gun is nothing to the arsenal they have. Help the ones that need to be helped and run down this road. There is a station at

the end of the street. Use my card to get through the security area, get on the train as quickly as possible. Do not talk to anyone, have this card out, wave it while everyone holds onto each other. You must hold on to each other as you go through the security area. This is the last train for the day, and we do not want to get stuck in this despicable place at night." I handed the lady I came to pick up my card. I know they heard those gunshots, and he's reached his group by now.

The ladies started making their walk to the station. I guess they weren't understanding the danger. When they heard the loud shouting coming from the other direction, it changed their pace. Damn Pops, you told me to pick up an employee, not get into a shootout with a whole fucking camp!

Chapter 5

Chaos in Gavian

"Damn Willy, you headed to that crappy ass bar?" Tony said as we drunk watered down drinks in front of the station. He was angry he didn't have enough money for the travel. I looked at him and just smiled while I took another gulp from my beer. It took me a while, but I now had enough money to make it to the Sanchi. The bar was on the outskirts, but it was one of the best bars I could go to in the galaxy. It wasn't the fanciest, but it has some of the best exotic drinks, and you meet many

people from around the universe. I haven't been in the past few years, since traveling is very expensive. Also, being from this crummy planet and it being an outcast from the already outcasted galaxy. I doubt I could ever get enough money to leave this galaxy, yet alone have the right documents to travel. So, the Sanchi is my paradise in this horrible place.

"When I get enough money to go myself, you will act just like me now. So I hope you remember this moment. If you even just split the train ticket, we could get drunk plenty of nights here. Why go all the way out there to spend a few days to just have a few drinks? How are you going to make it back, anyway? I know you don't have enough money for a round-trip." He was right, but it was well worth it to spend all this money to get away from this place every once in a while. It made him angry not being able to go. It felt like paradise listening to his frustration while smiling, waiting for the conductor to get on the intercom. I was ready to board and start my journey to relaxation. I felt a minor disappointment that he would not be coming. Having a companion with me was good for extra protection. This would not be my first time going by myself, but every time I go by myself, crazy things seem to happen. I

hope there will be no issues on this trip.

Loud shouting and noise came from the direction of the dirty Ca'Vais camps. They always started some type of trouble around here because of the weak security. I'm so glad I'm getting away from here for a couple of days. I hate it here with all these crummy camps and refugees from other places. The shouting

now turned into gunshots. People around me started looking down in the noise's direction. Shops started closing and locking the doors. The gunshots got louder and louder. This meant that whatever was happening was coming this way. I looked over at Tony. Both of us were frightened, as we both heard the gun shots not stopping but getting closer and closer. The security officer started looking around in panic, not knowing what to do. We knew he didn't want to get in a firefight being outgunned and out-manned. People started walking fast to the security area of the train station. If they could get past the security area, the rounds that would start flying everywhere wouldn't be able to pass through. Good thinking, I thought, getting up following them. I didn't want to get caught up at the back of the line when the problem would get here.

"Well, Tony, I guess that's the sound for me to get the fuck out of here. You need to do the same and be careful in this shit hole." While I was talking, four injured females appeared, heading toward the station. One pulled out a card, making her way through the security area without having to wait in line. I wish I had a card like that. I guess it's some type of kidnapping going on, but it doesn't look like the kidnappers got their victims. The station attendant let them through, shocked they had a card with that much access. He couldn't stop them, with them holding that card. It wasn't rare to see something like this happening. The sad part is they never get away. I remember a person almost made it onto the train but got shot in the back, dying by the door. A person paid for a ticket to get past the security area with a weapon. He shot him and walked right back out of the station. The security officer saw everything but would not do a thing. He knew that it would have been trouble to do something. The criminals run this area so he wouldn't be able to live on this planet anymore. This place is violent to where id cards from here get denied everywhere, making it so difficult to leave. I wish I could buy a forgery id card, but even that price is too much.

I made my way to the security line, which now was long. I was still dreaming about what I would do if I had one of those cards when another female walked up from the direction where the other four had come from. The gunfire had subsided by now, and she was holding a weapon in the open. She looked familiar, but I couldn't place where. She got in line like everything was normal, but kept looking back with the gun still in her hand. No one said a thing to her, seeing the blood

that was still on her face. The security officer did his best not to look in her direction, either. You could see the sweat dripping down his face.

Finally, I made it safely past the security area with no problems. I looked back at the female, who was only questioned for a second and allowed to walk through with the weapon still in her hand. She either has a lot of money or is some type of big shot. It's easy to bribe an employee to get through, but to have a weapon out is another thing. As soon as she cleared the security area, a couple of dangerous looking people walked up to the security area. Glad I had passed the area before they showed up. Now I can watch things from I hope a safe distance. Things weren't looking too good for the females now, but maybe because they are past the security area, they are clear. If this train was going to move, I was going to be on it no matter what happens. I do not get that many chances to leave this place, and these people will not ruin my opportunity. I know I will not get a refund or another ticket if I miss this train. The Sanchi is worth it even if I get shot by a stray round.

SECUR

TY AREA

Chapter 6

Why on my Day?

Okay, I know for a fact that I have bad luck. I knew seeing that beautiful Ca'Vais get off the ship earlier today that there were going to be problems. Now I'm hearing weapons going off in the distance, and everyone is looking at me to do something. The best advice I can give them is to get out of here. It's ridiculous for these people to think I would risk my life for them. Do they think I get paid well? I wouldn't even get any type of reward for saving anyone here. They would put me in more dangerous spots, thinking I like this crap. All I want to do now is go home and eat.

Now, it seems some group of females who have a special access card to get past security are rushing by. The only way they could have something like that was that damn bar girl. Trouble seems to happen everywhere she goes. That bar, Catalina, whatever you call it, brings a lot of the unwanted folks to this galaxy. It sounds pretty tempting right about now, though.

Not too long after the females get past the security area, the damn bar girl makes her appearance. To make matters worse, she has a weapon in hand, knowing that they banned weapons in this galaxy. Why is this happening while I'm at work? Not like I'm going to do anything about it. My pay isn't enough for me to risk my life. I will look the other way and ignore everyone looking at me. I'm just here until I'm off. If I stand back and act like I see nothing, I can get this day over with and head home to relax.

As the bar girl makes her way pass the security area, a caravan of vehicles arrive. I quickly made my way to the other side of the building, closer to the security area, just in case I had to run. I knew I would have to drop my weapon before I walked through, but this weapon wouldn't keep me alive if things went bad. Everyone watched as I made my move away from the front. That stupid drunk Willy was already past the security area watching all this crap unfold. He seems to have saved up enough money to head to that damn Catalina. He doesn't have anywhere else to go. I should be pestering him about stupid nonsense instead of dealing with a crazy, well-armed group. That's above my paygrade. Signing up to become a security officer was a very dumb idea. I thought I was going to make my family proud by getting involved in the government. I was hoping I could make a difference to this galaxy. This place will never change; the corruption has hardened.

I'm now sweating bullets, hoping that this will calm itself down without me getting involved. The group made its way toward the security area. The security guards, who hadn't been doing anything this whole time, kept looking at customer tickets, ignoring the situation, same as me. Now they were looking in my direction and waving me over, wanting help. I could see all this from the corner of my eye. I ignored them, hoping they would give up. It was working until a person decided it was his time to help by getting my attention for them. I hate this place so damn much! Looking at my non-existent watch, seeing it was time to go, I glanced over at the security guards, letting them see my non-existent watch face. Not waiting for their response, I made my way to my exit. I was clear and didn't want to get involved in any of that crap. I don't want to play big man.

As I was trying to leave, someone grabbed my shoulders from behind. A person came from the door while another jumped over the side rail. One rammed a weapon into my side, while the other pushed me toward the security area. The group I had been watching now were pointing and looking at the bar girl. She was

looking back at them, but past the security area.
"Look, I'm off. There is nothing I can do about any
of this. Just let me go because I hate this job." I didn't

care about showing my fear. I just wanted to be out of this situation and be able to go home. The only thing that was running through my mind at the moment was this being my last day on this planet. I wish I could have even seen pictures of another galaxy. The stories I heard from travelers make their crappiest places seem like paradise, compared to here. I was born in a horrible galaxy. Thoughts and memories of my life started flashing through my head. I had had no happiness in life, and now I was going to die over nothing.

"Look, this will all be over when we get our property back. Once that happens, we will be on our way. Also, we can't kill you without having to pay some money to the government for killing an employee. It's not worth it, so you will be cool if all goes the way it is supposed to go." The one with the gun still having it shoved in my back said. We were now close enough to hear the leader saying the same thing about property to the bar girl. I wanted to yell at the girl to give them the damn property so we can all be on our way. On this planet, it is a common practice to own people as property. I would not die today for these stupid females that came here. They should have known what they were getting themselves into. Make matters worse. Another group

of vehicles was now approaching the area. More come
onto the scene with weapons and I see an emblem,
meaning they are pirates. I looked back at the two
holding me hostage and saw fear in their eyes. No one
wanted to get in a battle with pirates, and it was the
Deadly Cove Pirates at that.

"Hey Tatiana, sorry, but we have a little… let's call this
a misunderstanding." A man with bright red hair walked
up to the leader of the other group. Both still were

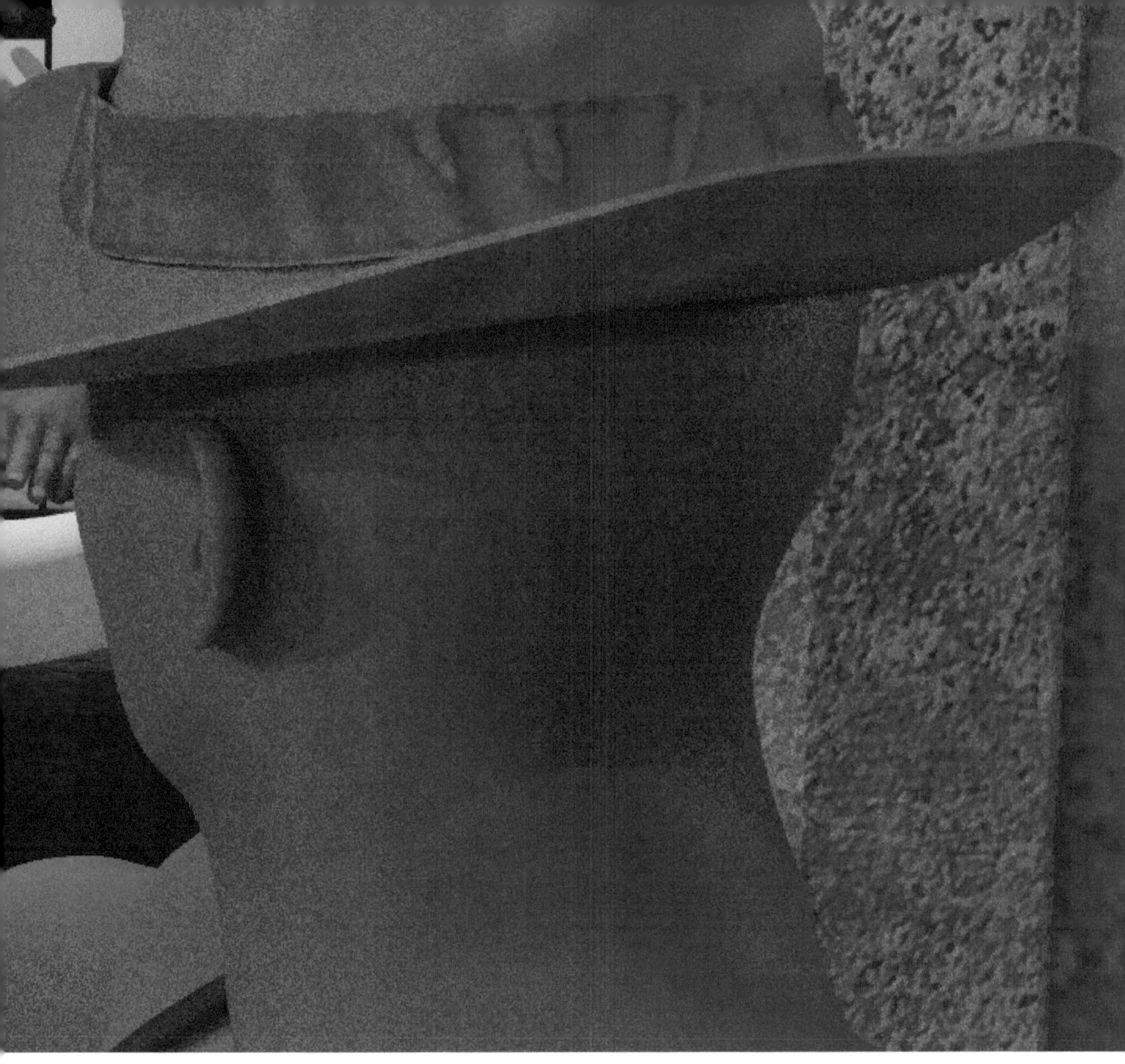

behind the security area while the bar girl stood a few distances on the other side. She could shoot them with no problem if they tried to run through the security area. It's programmed to only let certain people with certain cards pass through. With special cards, you can even pass with weapons and other devices. The government doesn't mention any of this to the security department. I don't understand why they won't give me a card so I can pass with my weapon. She must have this all

planned out; wish she could have told me. I could have taken the rest of the day off and avoided all this. How that bar girl has a special card perplexes me.

One of the pirate leader's men pushed the other group's leader, knocking him to the ground. He was being completely ignored and didn't want to have any problems with these pirates. Glancing over at the two behind me, he gave them a signal. They let me go and walked to their vehicles quickly. Didn't take long for them to be completely out of sight. The pirates

had now even stopped the train from departing by grabbing the conductor. For them to have access cards to the conductor was a total shock to me. What is my government doing giving out cards to these pirates? I'm going to call in sick tomorrow if I somehow survive this. I started taking small backwards steps, not trying to be noticed. Everyone's attention was now toward the security area. It's time for me to get out of here.

Chapter 7

Avian

"Look, Tatiana, we have a problem here. One of those females you helped escaped belongs to us and we want her back. You know this is business, so you can have the other women for wasted time. They are not our property, and we are generous businesspeople." I looked over at the conductor to check if he was okay. I didn't want to rough him up, since he transports a lot of our illegal shipments here. The security officer who was being held hostage also should see that I'm not like the scum that live on this planet.

Tatiana sure has caused a lot of problems for those Ca'Vais, but that isn't my concern. I don't see the other females, but my guess is they are on the train. Tatiana stood near one of the train doorways, using it as a defense. Her weapon pointing at me. She knew the round wouldn't be able to get past the security area. She had a weapon pointed at me, and I didn't like that. I took a couple of steps closer to the security area, but not close enough to get disintegrated. I still didn't have a card or ticket to walk in. Tatiana was in a nice defensive position tand wasn't budging.

Those people at that bar got to have military backgrounds or something. They are all fighters ready for any firefight if need be. I looked over at the

computer managing the security area. Funny how common people don't realize these things weren't built to prevent crime. They are for criminals who transport items on their transportation systems. They know we need our weapons, so we will pay for cards and anything that will allow us to travel with our weapons. "Sorry, Avian, I will not do that. I understand she is your property, but I will not let this go down today. Maybe we can work out some type of deal." Not lowering her weapon, she said, knowing that if this was another day, she would have agreed. She knows she is outgunned and outnumbered. Why is she putting her life on the line for people I know she doesn't know? She isn't the type of person to do something like this. "Tatiana, I know I don't know you that well. I enjoy

going to the Catalina and drinking there, so we have
had a few conversations. It's a significant rule that I
abide by where no one can attack each other or bring
weapons into the bar. But we're not there and this, you
can say, is my domain. We don't have any rules like
that here, and you know that. So why are you acting
so weird right now? Why are you putting your life on
the line for these females that you don't know? You
and I know Ca'Vais go for a good price on the street.
We had this one for a while now. We have a right to
want what is ours. This is theft of our property and I

know you don't like thieves. Don't be a thief, Tatiana."
She smirked, holding in laughter at hearing my last
sentence. Talking about thieves made her laugh, being
that I'm a leader of a pirate group. We rob businesses
for a living.

This was getting me nowhere. One of my men
now had a ticket for me to pass the security area. She
saw the hand off and knew she had little time left.
I was losing my temper with all this. We showed a
tremendous show of force in front of the traffickers.
If they come back with numbers, we won't stand a
chance. It's only five of us right now and backup won't
come until tomorrow. Glad they don't know that, but
we do not have time to be fooling around with this bar
girl.

"Look, Tatiana, I don't have all day. Hand over the one called Jasi, and the rest of you can go. If you don't accept this, I will kill everyone here and drag all the females with me." My ticket allowed me to cross the area with my weapon out. I was going to fire my weapon with my body still in the area, shielding me from her rounds. This has gone too far, and I want my property back now. She was a cool bartender, but this will be her last day alive. She should have never crossed paths with me outside that bar.

"Avian, you don't want to do this. My boss will be very upset if I don't make it back to work and you know that. How about we go back to the Catalina and talk about this some more? You don't want to be here, and I don't want to be here, either. It stinks around here. Is that your people that give off that foul odor?" She smiled, still not moving from her position. I've had enough of this and her. I don't care about her boss. When I see him, I'm going to kill him too and all his stupid employees. I aimed my gun at her, heading into the security area. I was about to squeeze the trigger when one of my men grabbed me. He almost lost his hand doing so.

"The Laop System Military has contacted us. I don't

know how they know our frequency. They instructed us to leave this galaxy immediately. I've contacted the others, and they have gone into hiding. This sounds real, and we should lie low. If we're going to leave this planet, we must go now." Gop was still listening to his headphones, getting more information. I looked back at Tatiana, who was smiling, knowing that her boss had to have something to do with this. How could he have known this was happening now? I know little about that man, but he has some crazy influence and contacts throughout the universe. It makes little sense for a person his age. I put my gun in its holster and smoothed back my hair. I took a deep breath, trying to hold back all my rage in wanting to kill this female standing in front of me. One of these days I'm going to kill you, Tatiana. I turned around and signaled my men to move out.

Chapter 8

The New Employees

I'm glad you always come through in the nick of time, Pops. Stretching out on the seat finally having this ordeal done felt good. Well, this was the start of it, but right now I can rest without having to look over my shoulder. The train started moving, taking us to the spaceport that will get us off this crappy planet.

There isn't anything special about this place. It doesn't even have drinkable water. The only way they survive is off the universal and the star system ports. If they didn't have those places, they wouldn't survive a day. Mountains and dirt are the only thing on this planet. Garbon isn't that great either, but the moons are quite nice. Many people call it the backwoods, but at least they don't look like this place.

Next stop I guess is Garbon, or the other moon Gostos, depending on the price. Once we get there, I will be more in my comfort zone. I know I will run into some pirates on this trip. I'm hoping if that happens, I will be closer to Mer. Mer, Garbon's moon, is where the Catalina is. On it, there are three sizable groups that control most of the land. We don't have any problems with any of them, but their conflicts are bad. We hear a lot of the stories about them at the bar. I have a safe passage through most of the areas. Once I get on there,

I will be safe from any pirates out to get me. I'm ready to have a drink myself, forget work.

Everyone on-board was still frightened of me and the females. My smile made them look away. The show was over, and they could get on with their lives. Nothing in this damn galaxy is important to me. I damn well don't care about some poor Neetois traveling on this dirty, crappy train. What do they even do here to afford a ticket on the train? One train that goes back and forth all day and night. This must be the people's

enjoyment because there isn't anything else here. Why live on a planet like this? I need a bath to get this stench off me. I closed my eyes, ready for some good rest before we get to the port.

"Who are you?" The pink and grey hair female finally built up enough courage to ask me. I cracked my eyes, a little sad I would not get my good rest. She was staring out the window with her sad eyes. She couldn't be looking at anything important. It was only dirt and rocks out there. If she is still thinking about the ordeal, she needs to get over it. It was something that many people do not escape from. She should be lucky. She's going to have to get stronger if she wants to live outside the Ca'Vais galaxy alone. I would be happy if someone rescued me from enslavement. With her being there, she saved three other females. They all seemed fine, but the two that have bruises had some scars that might be permanent. Other than that, they all look fine. They were going to live, which was all that mattered.

"I assume you're the one that I'm here to pick up for the Catalina. My boss is always mysterious, so I didn't have any information about what you looked like. The idiot boss told me about this very late. Oh yeah, who is Jasi? You will probably have a bounty on your head in this galaxy. It won't be bigger than mine, though." Avian was not finished with me in the slightest. Having a female best him was not something he would be okay with. Him coming to the bar a lot is going to be very awkward going forward. How is it going to be the next time he shows up? We had no problems, but he had a huge temper. I guess it wasn't wise to get on his angry side. Now I'm going to see how angry he can really get.

As I was in my thoughts thinking about how angry Avian was right now. Jasi jumped up in a panic. I'm guessing it was hitting her, the bounty on her head. Looking at how beautiful she is, I can see why they want her back.

"I shouldn't have gone with you people! I don't want to die! I never should have come here in the first place!" She was now in an uncontrollable shake.

"Look, you can work at the bar. Pops loves pretty females no matter what situation you're in. It's not the best place in the world, but you will be protected once you are inside the city walls. Oh sorry, was in my thoughts. My name is Tatiana and I'm going to be your senior at the Catalina. What is your name, new employee? I need to call you something besides pink and grey hair."

"My name is Viviana, and I don't want to work here. I want to go back home. I'm not ready to be in a new galaxy or work in a place like this. This is too much for me." Tears fell down her face. She still looked out the window. What has the Ca'Vais government been doing these past years? Sending ladies here not prepared for the societies they will face is very unwise. Especially coming here to Neetoi, which is a cesspool for male Ca'Vais. Something isn't right in their government right now.

"Look! both of you don't have enough money to make it back to Ca'Vais. That's the end of that. I'm shocked you had enough money and special clearances to make it here. This is one of the most dangerous areas for female Ca'Vais. Both of you don't look like you have one bit of military experience. Why would they clear you two to come here? If you two stay with me and give me a percentage of your pay, I will let you live with me and help you settle here. You two also can come to work and live with me." The other two weren't Ca'Vais, so I figured they wouldn't need to work at the Catalina.

"We're both from Laop and going to the embassy to

get our identification cards to get back home. They wouldn't let us leave that area, and we didn't have any way of escaping. Thank you so much for rescuing us. I know you didn't have to do it and now you have a bounty on your head. They treat us worst then the female Ca'Vais because we don't go for that much compared to them. They were going to kill us for pleasure if you hadn't rescued us today. Thank you again." One of them was very grateful while shaking my hand, thanking me. I didn't want to be rude and ask for money, which I knew they didn't have. Viviana and Jasi said nothing, remaining quiet.

Remembering that I was able to get Viviana's book, I handed it to her. She grabbed it, not thanking me or looking in my direction. She kept looking out the window. I will take a fee out of her first paycheck for that. I don't know why they look so bummed when I saved their lives. They would have been sex slaves if I hadn't come around. Now I have trouble with these pirates, but I'm not crying and worried. We must get to Mer and then we will be safe. I wonder who is working right now? I know the boss isn't. I closed my eyes, ready for my nap. Weapon was still in my hand, wishing I had brought more weapons.

Chapter 9

Bartender Duties Today

"Look, I have been waiting for some time for my drink. I'm ready to get drunk. Why are you still taking your time trying to cook food for that idiot? You better get your act together, Hector, before you lose this nice tip." Grevo said to me, acting like he was going to give me a tip. I ignored him and continued making the food. Where in Mer are you Tata!? No one told me she was going to pick up a new employee. Pops didn't bring in anyone either to help. He was acting like he was going to come to the rescue. That man does nothing

if a woman doesn't ask him. With him not even being here or giving me any help, I'm the cook and bartender for the day. I'm also the security, having to monitor everyone. People are trying to run out on the bill. I can't wait for this day to end, but it just started.

"Damn, can you cook this a little faster? You are taking forever!" Another customer said over my shoulder, right next to me. This is ridiculous having to do all this and now have a customer come into the kitchen and watch me cook. I need a vacation.

"Look, can you take your ass back to your seat? You're not even supposed to be back here. You can eat somewhere else if you don't want to wait. That's for everyone here! If you don't want to wait, take your asses down to the next place!" I screamed at the top of my lungs. Everyone got quiet for a second, then burst

into laughter. I don't even know why I even tried. "Stop joking. You know this is the only spot that is the safest and has pretty alright food. I traveled all the way out here for the entertainment and the beautiful women. But when I get here, I don't see any beautiful women here except your slow chef ass. You're going to be my

entertainment for today, I guess. So, feel great about us complaining to you about what you are messing up on and taking forever on. Once all the women get back from wherever they are, no one will pay any attention to you anymore. By the way, I'm entertained by your facial expressions." Grevo said, somehow now eating from a plate of food. Where did he get that food? I noticed someone in the corner, scared to look up, and realized he had taken it from another customer. The guards prohibited violence within the city walls, but people must leave this land by closing hours. If I would say anything, it would be bad for that person, but gave Grevo a stern look, which he smiled and laughed. I don't know why I work here.

"Hey Hector, I heard there is going to be a new girl coming to work here. It would be great to see more beautiful women here. Tata is cool, but she's very aggressive and mean. Trish sometimes comes to work, and Melinda is a damn monster. Yea, she's a bombshell but worst then Tata. I don't know how you could work with her. I thought lady Ca'Vais were nice and gentle, but that one is always ready to tear your head off." An object came flying, hitting Grevo straight in the face, knocking him out cold.

"Grevo. You know Melinda is at work today. I wouldn't say rude things about her." I wanted to finish with when she's here but didn't want to get hit with whatever she had near her. Her being here is worst since I must clean up after her, while also do her work. She does work, sometime. Tata gets her to do something every odd day. Some days she comes in a very cheerful mood, still does nothing, but is better to be around. Today I guess she's reading a book, and into the story, because I

97

haven't talked to her much.

Melinda's attitude has calmed down since her first day here. She still has a strong hatred for males, no matter where they come from. She has been getting a little cooler with me since I've been feeding her, and she likes the way I cook. If I didn't cook well, she would have murdered me or got me fired by now. I really feel she would have killed me. Tata once told me she was in the military for Ca'Vais, but something happened, and she fled here. I didn't get into it any deeper because every employee has some type of past and it's not good to dig up old wounds.

Everyone that works here has some type of reason to be working so far on the outskirts of this galaxy.

Tata is also very mysterious. No one knows where she comes from, but she knows a lot about many galaxies. I'm guessing she was some type of Laop security intelligence officer. She probably had to go into hiding. We have a strong Laop military presence around this planet, but with the wars here on Mer, they keep their distance. That would make this a great place to hide from the Laop authorities, but still be in the star system. To stay out of the public eye, a lot of government and criminal organizations hold meetings here. It's not a simple task to get to this city, though.

Once you get here, you don't have to worry about someone killing you within these walls. Inside these city walls, no one cares who you are. Everyone treats you with some form of respect. You might not get the best respect, but better than outside these walls. Guests within these walls can only stay for up to ten days. They must leave or the city wall guards will arrest them.

"I'm about to take a nap." Melinda said, walking by. It still is a pleasure to have her around. She is exquisite and smells great. Even with her mean glare, she's still very attractive.

"Stop daydreaming about her and finish making the damn drinks!" someone yelled from the angry crowd, who were all growing impatient. No one said anything about the other employee going to take a nap. They knew not to say anything about her.

Chapter 10

Viviana's Diary

Page 2- I hate this place!

That is what I think about this place, seeing nothing but wickedness here. I regret doing that stupid bet and coming here. I left my universe to come and almost got raped by a male Ca'Vais. All of this, I could've never even imagined. Growing up, never seeing one, now coming to a freaking camp full of them. This is definitely the worst place in the universe. Being with a dangerous female too, who just killed a couple of people, now taking me to my job like this is nothing new. Thinking that I would work right now seems so far-fetched.

Still not even close to the planet of this bar. I don't have any money to turn around and go home. Wouldn't even dare staying here by myself waiting for a ship. I'm thankful that this crazy female rescued me. She should've come on time, though; I wouldn't have been in that situation. I don't think I'm going to like her. She has been bragging about herself the whole time before falling asleep with her weapon on her lap. Who is more dangerous? Her? Or the pirates? She's conning us, but we don't have any choice. Being protected by her was the best bet right now for my survival.

I must write about the way the people stood around as I was being kidnapped. A security officer watched the

whole event, but he acted like he had nothing to do with the situation. I'm never going to forget his face, seeing it while I was being carried away. I hope that is the last show of violence I'm going to see for a while.

Tatiana is the name of the crazy female, by the way. She shot a male in the face. Seeing it explode is something I never want to see again. I can't believe she can sleep after doing something like that. This place seemed somewhat peaceful, seeing the interactions with the males and females in the beginning. Now, after seeing this much violence and the nature of these people, I'm ready to go back home. I'm now imprisoned to work for this Pops and his Catalina, since I don't have any money to get back home. I'm terrified of going anywhere without this crazy lunatic woman by my side now.

The train hits a spot on our journey where all the windows go black, and an announcement comes over the intercom. "Reaching Laop classified areas. All areas past this point are prohibited from viewing. Once we reach the end of the classified area, the windows will change to transparent." It was repeated twice. Even though the intercom was loud, Tatiana slept right through. I guess she's accustomed to it, since this

wasn't her first time here, I guess.

The train we are riding in is an ancient model from my standards. I didn't even think it could go at this speed it's going without falling apart. Some of the technology on this planet looks ancient and corroded. There are no structures outside of the port I came from. Well, from what I could see.

It has been a while now, and the train hasn't made any stops. The port was very nice, but outside of the place, it was old and run down. Tent shacks and a couple of buildings were all around the primary port building, but nothing had two stories. They didn't seem to have the knowledge to build, and all this technology was from other galaxies. Laop seems to have a firm hold on this planet. Chances are this technology comes from them.

It's funny with all that is going on. I've realized I still know nothing about the Catalina. What type of work will I be doing? This will be my first time working at a bar. Back home, I was learning how to be a news reporter. I hope I'm able to do the tasks they want me to do. The way things look here, if I don't work out, Pops will sell me to those Ca'Vais to get his money back. I assume he paid for my ticket, but I

don't know why he would. If they have these sex slave groups, they could easily find someone that could be a bartender. They wouldn't have to look in another galaxy.

The other two that Tatiana rescued seemed to be okay people. There is a Ca'Vais named Jasi that seems to have been here for a while, but not that long. Someone conned her into coming here for a modeling and entertainment career. She thought she was going to travel, and her family had the money. She felt like it was an opportunity to see the universe; I guess. Now she is going to be working with me and living with me too at this place. Pirates chasing and putting a huge bounty on your head must mean you are some special person.

I felt Jasi was some sort of leader, but she looks like a totally different person now. She keeps crying in her hands. I wish I could say something to make her feel better. There wasn't anything I could say that would make things better. I was going through my problems, too. We are all in a horrible place and in a horrible situation I don't think we're going to get out of. We should have never come to this place. The other two females were going back home once we got to the port. Their galaxy has some sort of program, which allows them to get a ticket back to their galaxy. I wish our government had something similar, so I could go back home now. The planet, Gavian, is nothing but a wasteland from what I have been able to see. I have seen no natural sources of water on this planet. Everything looks like it gets shipped here.

We are heading to a planet named Garbon, or its moon Gostos, once we get to the spaceport. I don't know what is up with Tatiana, but she wouldn't give me a straight answer. She wants to keep a low profile because of the pirate incident. I suspect that she's trying to find the cheapest flight. I have realized this Tatiana is very cheap and only cares about money. If we were not giving her money from our paychecks, she would have already abandoned us by now. Also, she even knows we're going to give her a piece of our paychecks unwilling because we don't want to turn up missing.

This place doesn't seem like it cares much about life. Tatiana is going to become wanted for killing those people. I know she's going to get some reward from this Pops for saving us. I am thankful she did, though. They were going to sell me off right before she came. Still, I do not have a great expectation of where I'm going. The only one I can trust right now is Jasi, but ever since we got on this train, she has not been herself. When I first met her at that place, she seemed strong and caring for everyone. She said she was going to look out for me, but now she is a frightened, pathetic excuse of how she was when I first met her. I hope she snaps out of it because we must help each other. The pirate group wanted Jasi and was going to do anything to get her back from the way I saw it. To even phantom something like that happening to me I couldn't think about. I hope nothing bad happens to her.

While we were in that house, she had told us she

had read a lot about the Neetoi galaxy from some forbidden books. Neetoi used to be a great galaxy long before I was born and before the Laop government took control of the system. The Ca'Vais galaxy war's intensity caused a lot of trade routes to close. Which affected the Neetoi galaxy tremendously. It is nothing like what it was back in the day. Jasi said that she got the book from her grandmother, who loved to learn about everyone's history.

Chapter 11

Train ride to Space Port

"So, what made you come to this awful place?" I couldn't take the silence anymore on the train. After Tatiana calmed down with her bragging, everything fell silent. My viewpoint was only for this day, so I wanted to know more about the people who have been here. "They offer you fake dreams. That's mainly what brought me here. I didn't know any better and someone paid for my ticket. These tickets to travel from one galaxy to another ain't cheap, so I thought it was a once in a lifetime dream. Having a horrible time since

I got here makes me no longer regret my galaxy. It will be difficult starting over, but it will be better than staying any longer here. I don't want anyone to ever know what happened to me here." The female with the red hair said. They wouldn't give their names. I didn't want to be rude and pry for it. Their culture probably

was why they didn't give it out. Tatiana was fast asleep
still having her weapon in hand, but her hand wasn't
near the trigger luckily. I didn't want it to go off by
accident. I can't believe she can sleep after everything
she did. Jasi still wasn't doing too well, but she had
calmed down a little. Still hadn't said a word, though.

The other female from Laop was asleep like Tatiana, but she would wake up in fright, then calm right back down, going back to sleep.

"I know little of her story. She was already there by the time I got there. I feel sorry that you cannot go home." She continued to talk. She wasn't that talkative at first, but I guess she's calming down more and feels like she's in a safe place.

"I thought this was going to be a dream come true for me. I thought I was going to have a lot of marvelous stories to tell my family when I got back. Now I don't think I'm going to make it back and I don't think I'm going to live like how Tatiana lives. Yeah, I wish I could leave right now. This is my first-time seeing death, and she looks and acts like this is normal. I'm not cut out for that type of stuff. I can't even see how this planet looks on this train ride. Why would they block the view?"

"So, no one sees how messed up this planet is. The entire planet has no natural water, but people are living on it. How do you think that works?" Tatiana spoke with her eyes still closed. She was listening to the conversation the whole time. She continued, "Just like this galaxy, this entire planet is corrupt. Right now, we should be passing by the Deadly Cove Pirate camp, or I should say fortress, how big that place is. This planet has tons of mysteries, even I don't know about, but at the end of the day, it is not worth living here."

"Why do you live here? You seem smart and strong enough to leave this place." The red hair female said to Tatiana.

"It's funny how you two think that any other galaxy differs from this place. Most people only pay attention to their insignificant lives, not looking at others. Don't think that there is a peaceful galaxy out there. It will only fool you. This is the real society that makes the universe move. Yes, this place stinks and has nothing of value, but everywhere you go, you will find some place like this. You make the most out of what you got. This is what I have, and you might find some hidden gems here if you search hard enough. Not on this planet, though. You two are traveling virgins. You two will learn about this place and about traveling. We still have a long way to go and, to be honest, I don't know how it's going to go once we get to the port."

"The killer talk like this place is like Ca'Vais. That makes little sense. It's nothing like Ca'Vais. You have never been to the galaxy, so how can you say my

home galaxy is something like this? You are lying to yourself or have lost your mind. I need to work and get enough money to leave this rotten, despicable place." Jasi finally broke her long silence. The room fell silent again. Tatiana said nothing back to her. I didn't know what to say and that reaction from Jasi made the red hair Laop fall silent again. The windows were still dark, so we couldn't see outside. It had been over two hours since they had darkened. When will we get out of this area?

"Nothing like Ca'Vais? You mean the galaxy where the males and females have been in a bloody war for centuries?" Tatiana laughed and then continued, "I kill to stay alive. I don't kill for joy. I don't want to be some prisoner where others can have at it with me. The universe has no rules, and you better learn that. I feel bad that they took you all from your nice, happy lives, because it surely seems like they kept you away from the dangers of even your home galaxy. Someone didn't place you here, but you got into a situation without thinking about it. If you want to be docile and become controlled by others, fine by me, but I'm not a person who will accept that. From my perspective, I'm the better person. I saved people today while you all were

the victims needed saving. I'm not staring into the ground, worried about some bounty on my head. You and I are in the same boat, and I have it harder. I must get you two to the bar and a job." Tatiana still had her eyes closed; she never once opened her eyes during the conversation. Jasi said nothing, staring at the ground. From Tatiana's answer, I guess that was the trigger to make the red hair stop talking altogether. I didn't want to break the silence, so I kept quiet, not knowing what to do, since I couldn't look out the window. Tatiana was feeling my uneasiness, and it was bothering her.

"Get some rest. We have a long way to go before we make it to the spaceport. Once we get there, it might be a while before we can get a good sleep, so I suggest you sleep as much as you can now." She laid out even more. Jasi laid back and closed her eyes with the Laop female doing the same. It was me, Tatiana, and Jasi on a long side of the seats, while the other two were on the other side. It was long enough for everyone to stretch out. I laid down, closing my eyes, still not feeling well from being in a new galaxy and the events that took place. Yesterday, I was so excited to see a new world. Now, I'm ready to go back and never leave my parents' home. I hope this is the worst I'm going to see here.

Chapter 12

Not my Day

This day has turned out to be a horrible one
for me. I was thinking to myself as we were doing
everything we could to get away from a Laop patrol
ship. The military call had to be fake, but it seems there
are real patrol ships in the area looking for something.
We didn't have any important shipments going out
today, so the activity can't be for us.

"Avian, I don't think it's a good idea to go back to the
primary base. We should have stayed at the Gavian
base, even if we would have been stuck there for a

while. There is no information about why they are here on any communication waves." Gop was trying his best to figure out what was going on. I didn't want to stay on that horrible planet any longer, so staying at that base was out of the question. He was right that it would not be a good idea to get back to the primary base in this galaxy. The Laop military had a secret base on the moon next to our secret moon base of the planet Slytia. We know about each other but still haven't found the exact location of each other bases. It would be hard to swing this ship under their radar toward the moon. Laop would figure out our exact location. Maybe they knew I would be on this planet today and wanted to catch me. I'm not that important to them for this big of a presence. All this is Tatiana's fault! All she had to do was turn over Jasi, and that would have been it. We would have gotten off the planet before these military ships got into the area. She's going to pay for this, eventually.

"Gop, make course toward Garbon. We're going to hide out around that planet for a while and monitor Tatiana and Jasi. We'll get Jasi back and kill Tatiana if she won't go with us too. With those stupid rules, we can't attack them in the city, but they haven't made it to the

moon yet. I don't think they even made it off, Gavian. With this much activity, it's bound to cause them delays at the spaceport." I walked over to the visual window, looking at Gavian. We navigated through more patrol ships using our cloaking devices to remain undetected. Luckily, this ship had the latest cloaking technology that we had stolen. They couldn't see us or detect us, but they could run into us, making it very difficult for us to maneuver. I don't know how my vice-captain could get this, but she comes through when the job needs completing.

"Do you think we can get her back before Tanya finds out?" Frank walked into the cockpit room, eating. He had a huge habit of always eating when we weren't fighting. He was right that I didn't want Tanya to find out about any of this. It's good having a great vice-captain, but she's always waiting for me to slip up and become the next leader. She is capable, but I will never let a female Ca'Vais lead me under any circumstances. She will be my loyal pet, but never my boss.

"Sorry, Avian, I told her the situation. She was the one who sent the data on the whereabouts of the patrol ships. We wouldn't have been able to get through this mini blockade without her help." Gop was one of my

best loyal men but would do anything for Tanya, which
made things horrible for me to trust him. Showing my
anger would make Gop see I was worried she might
take my spot. Frank was the only one who knew she
was trying. I don't even know if people would accept
her or fight against her if she tried to take my spot. I
don't want to think anything about a war with her right
now. There is too much money being made, and our
influence is strong. If we keep this going, we are all
going to be set for the rest of our lives.

"That's okay Gop, I didn't want to make us look bad.
If we catch her though, it won't be a problem and she
will not have any chance to laugh at us." Before I could
finish, I saw Gop was wanting to tell me more news.
"She knew you would say that and said she would
handle the whole situation of getting Jasi back. I think
it would be easier for her to persuade Jasi to come
back since she is a Ca'Vais herself. I didn't tell her
the female we have problems with was Tatiana. She
will find out when she goes to the bar." I should have
known Gop was going to tell her everything. I didn't
want Tanya to be going around that bar. This day keeps
getting better and better. Once we hit a good opening
and hit light-speed, I will have time to get some rest and

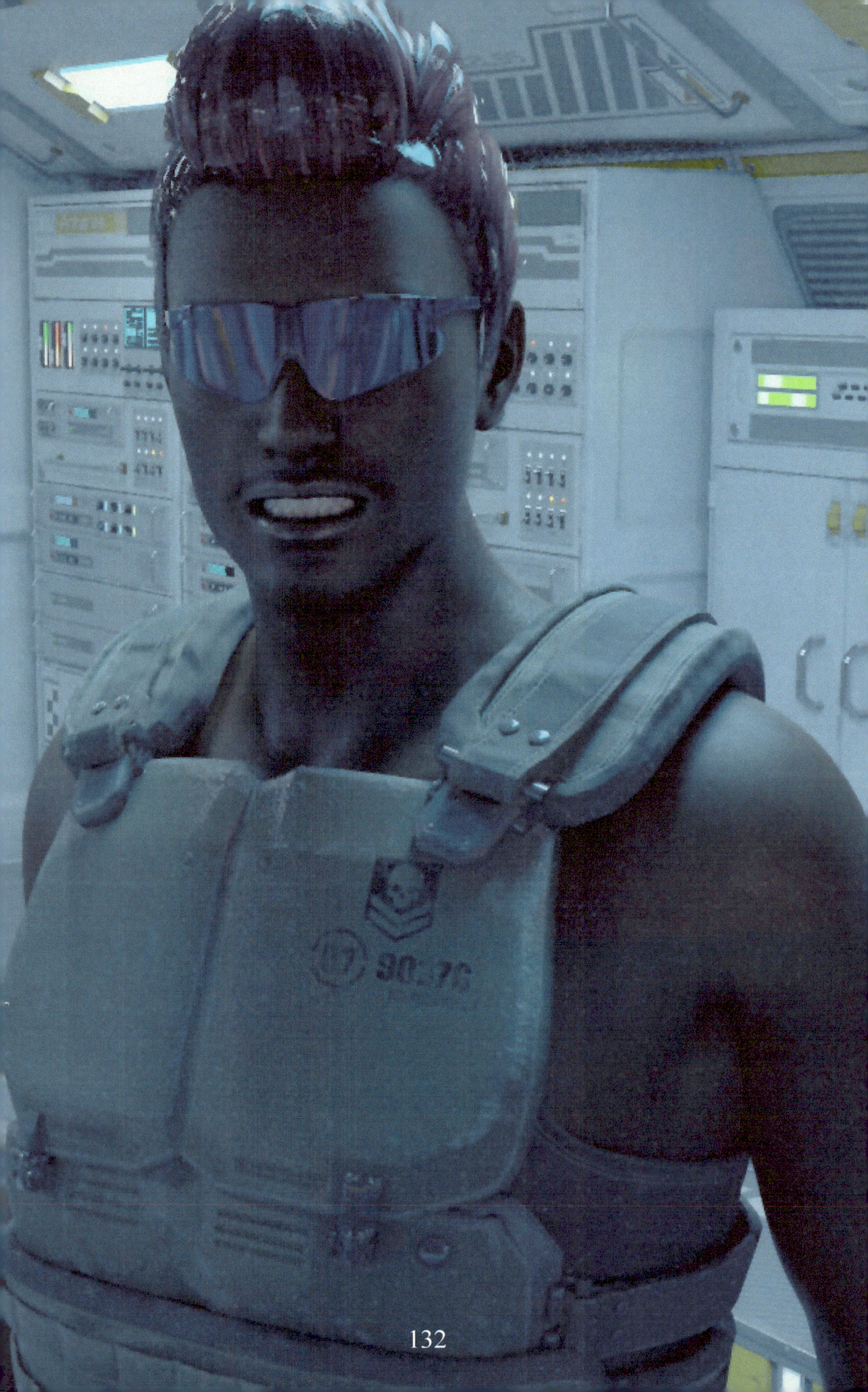

tomorrow will be a lot better. Frank stood in the corner eating something else, not having a care in the world.

It was a pain to maneuver through the blockade of military ships, but we were finally floating in deep space. Using our engines now would have still got us spotted from this distance. We floated along, watching for any ship coming at a fast speed not to bump into us. "Good thing you didn't tell her about Tatiana. Tanya should be coming from the primary base, so we will make it there before her. I can have the situation all under control by the time she arrives."
"She said you would say that. She also said you can do whatever you want, but understand she is going to be the one that will get Jasi back." Gop said, giving me the x signal that he had nothing else to say. Tanya was doing what she wanted again and showing that she could get the job done when she can. The problem is how she flaunts and wants to be the big guy. I should let her catch Jasi because I don't care about her as much as I care about killing Tatiana now. I need to figure out if there is some group there that can kill Tatiana with no one knowing.

Flos Spacelines
Relax while we take
you to your destination
Flos Spacelines
The best Space Service in the
Neetoi Galaxy
We travel to near galaxies also
for the Neetoi Galaxy. Check us
out on the space web!